JUST ANOTHER BOOK

BY A. NOBODY

John H. Sanders

ISBN 979-8-89112-131-7 (Paperback)
ISBN 979-8-89112-132-4 (Digital)

Covenant Books
11661 Hwy 707
Murrells Inlet, SC 29576
www.covenantbooks.com

INTRODUCTION

I want to thank you for discovering this book.
I hope you will give it more than just a quick look.

For this is not a book you read straight through,
But wherever you open it, may the perfect chapter find you.

And within that chapter, may you always find,
God's hope, strength, comfort, and peace of mind.

No doubt there will be a sentence or two—
Where you'll ask yourself—Can that really be true?

If that should ever happen to you,
Ask, Seek, and Knock for this is what
	The Lord would have you do!

PROLOGUE

In an endeavor to combine patriotism, politics, and God, three things that should *never* be discussed are very challenging. However, I will make the attempt. Included will be a couple of "experiencing God" moments of my own.

In my opinion, the three words that best depict the world today are "THE TWILIGHT ZONE!"

A while back, I watched an old TV show titled *The Twilight Zone.* So from the program, I would like to quote Rod Serling, who introduces and gives insight into "what you are about to see," in this case, read.

You walk into a room at your own risk because it leads to the future—not a future that will be, but one that might be. This is not a new world. It is simply an extension of what began in the old one.

It has patterned itself after every dictator who has ever planted the ripping imprint of a boot on the pages of history since the beginning of time! It has refinements, technical advances, and a more sophisticated approach to the destruction of human freedom. But like every one of these superstates that preceded it, it has one iron rule: "LOGIC IS AN ENEMY, AND TRUTH IS A MENACE!"

It was titled "The Obsolete Man," with the basic premise—human extinction! It made me think of our world today, where "leaders" of socialism, communism, Marxism, and all forms of governmental totalitarianism threaten freedom of thought, expression, and words in general.

The history of these aforementioned *isms* has also shown that economic inflation usually, if not always, leads to a recession, which leads to depression. And cemented strong within these *isms* is that there is no room for God! And from that comes the spirit of the Antichrist!

These so-called leaders seem to continually encourage themselves in devising evil! They will keep lists. Traps will be secretly set. They will say to each other, No one can catch us. No one can detect our perfect crime! And of course, all the while taking potshots at God!

But most Americans and Christians here and around the world believe our nation, our America, is led by God. Through prayer and voting, our leaders have the privilege to sit in seats of authority. Their assignment should not only be to listen to, serve, and answer to America's citizens but also to have a greater obligation and responsibility to listen to, serve, and answer to God, Who says, "Vengeance is mine!"

In times of trouble, Americans, pray! That time has come!

CHAPTER 1

In the Beginning

I've been thinking! Thinking about my own thoughts and the thoughts of others! What are we thinking? More importantly, what are we hearing? And to whom are we listening?

For US, as Americans and as Christians, I hear a battle cry! For this is our hour to pray and prepare for spiritual battle—spiritual warfare.

Our assignment is to bring to life those of US who are spiritually DEAD so as to come ALIVE in the Holy Spirit! For is it not written, "In the last days, I will pour out My Spirit on all flesh"? And what will it look like when the Spirit comes?

It will be OUR time to GROW and SHINE His light!

It will be OUR time to HEAL where there are killings!

It will be OUR time to BUILD UP those who are broken down!

It will be OUR time to BURY our laughter and cry about the world's plight!

It will be OUR time to STOP partying and feel spiritually sick about our behavior!

It will be OUR time to PUT TOGETHER those who have been torn inside!

It will be OUR time to SPEAK THE TRUTH, where we have shunned our duty in silence!

It will be OUR time to LOVE where there is hate!

It will be OUR time to PRAY for the Lord's peace and coming, so war will be no more!

It will be OUR time to LIVE in Him and to DIE to self!

God's plan of attack is that we never war against people but by His blood, and in the Name of Jesus, we pray and do spiritual battle against powers and principalities, rulers of darkness, and spiritual wickedness in high places! Always remember that our weapons are not physical weapons. For our God and His Word are mighty in the bringing down of any and all strongholds, which includes addictions!

One last detail. We must be willing to share in His sufferings if we are to share in His glory!

OUR PRAYER. Father, we cannot win any battles in our own might or power, but by Your Spirit, all things are possible! Cleanse us as individuals and as a nation. Continue to grant us the ability to pray openly and invite and prompt our leaders to seek Your guidance as we ask You to forgive US our sins. We ask You to begin to pour out Your Holy Spirit across America—this One Nation Under Your domain! In Jesus's Name, we pray!

JUST ANOTHER CHAPTER 2

Common Sense was a pamphlet written by Thomas Paine in 1776. From the booklet, he quotes Giacinto Dragonetti, who served as Italian consul of Sicily and eventually became the president of the Royal Court of Sicily.

> The science of the politician consists in fixing the true point of happiness and freedom. Those men would deserve the gratitude of ages, who should discover a mode of government that contained the greatest sum of individual happiness, with the least national expense.

Paine goes on, quoting Dragonetti on virtue and rewards.

> But where say some, is the King of America? I'll tell you. He reigns above and does not make havoc on mankind like the Royal Brute of Britain (King George, Pharaoh of England).
>
> Yet that we not appear to be defective even in earthly honors, let a day be sol-

emnly set apart for proclaiming the charter; let it be brought forth on the divine law, The Word Of God. Let a crown be placed thereon, by which the world may know that so far as we approve of a monarchy, that in America, *the law is king.*

For in absolute governments, the King is LAW, so in free countries, the *law* ought to be King; and there is to be no other. But lest any ill use should afterward arise, let the crown at the conclusion of the ceremony be demolished, and scattered among the people whose right it is.

From The Book Of Books—The Bible—Ecclesiastes 12:13–14 (NKJV) says,

Let us hear the conclusion of the whole matter. Fear God and keep His Commandments, for this is the duty of everyone. For God will bring every work into judgement, including every secret thing and hidden intent, whether good or evil!

JUST ANOTHER CHAPTER 3

So you say you want a revolution! How about a revelation?

I'm not sure what "wordsmith" is in charge of formulating and changing word definitions today, but I have a couple of words I'd like to redefine. The two words—*right* and *left.*

I'd like to think that the definition of "the right" is a belief that God, the Father of Jesus, watches over our nation by means of the Holy Spirit.

I'd like to think that the definition of "the left" is a belief that money is god, and the spirits of other gods and goddesses have come into our land, hoping to hammer "The Final Nail" in Christianity.

America has a directional problem! And with the spirit of the Antichrist hovering over many parts of our nation, no wonder many of her citizens are lost, dazed, and confused. So the big question, spiritually and politically speaking, is, Which way should we go?

As our Republican and Democrat leaders "slug it out," and perhaps before America falls to one of the *isms,* I'm thinking, *What would Presidents Washington and Lincoln have to say if they were alive today? What would their State of the Union address look and sound like?*

Now both presidents, being familiar with the Bible, understood that, in truth, any nation divided against itself will fall! No doubt, this is something that every world leader knows, and today, some of those world leaders looking and salivating over America are "Banking" on it!

So what would these two God-fearing men do? What should every president of this "one nation under God" say or do? Standing in front of many cameras and microphones for the first time, "I'd like to think," both would echo the same words: "My fellow Americans, now is the time to pray!"

With eyes closed, heads bowed, and hands folded, "I'd like to think," they would address the nation something like this:

Our dear Heavenly Father, as the people of these United States, we come before You in true humility. We recognize You as the real Father of our nation, and we ask that You forgive us for our many sins. For we somehow have gone off course and have wandered from Your path in so many ways. At times, we have made a total about face and have gone in the opposite direction. So for this, as individuals and on behalf of our nation, we not only ask for forgiveness but also for Your mercy as well.

Not since the Civil War has America had so much fighting from within and been so divided. One of our darkest hours. Yet today, once again, there are killings in the streets, and we are slaughtering each other with back-biting and vicious accusations and are ever so divided!

Father, we need more than our own wisdom and logic to overcome the spirit of the Antichrist that is playing havoc around the world. In ourselves, we can do nothing short of bloodshed! So we ask that You intervene.

Please send to us a latter-day rain of Your Holy Spirit. May He lead us and guide us back to Your Ways. For though it appears our nation is walking through a valley of the shadow of death, help us not to fear any evil! For we trust and believe You are with us and for us. And by Your Spirit, You will protect us and comfort us.

Give us Your plan concerning this internal conflict— this division, which sounds and feels like a sledgehammer banging on our walls until it finally crushes our nation in two! By Your Spirit, mend us together. For it is You to whom "We Put Our Trust!"

Yes, revolution is in the air across America! But from You, Father, one revelation can turn a revolution into a revival! May it be so. In Jesus's Name! Amen!

Following the prayer is a reading from the Bible, in Psalm 46 (NKJV). Here are the first two and the last two verses from the reading.

> God is our refuge and our strength,
> A very present help in trouble. Therefore
> we will not fear, Even though the earth be
> removed.

> Be still, says the Lord, and know
> that I AM GOD; I will be exalted among

the nations, I will be exalted in the earth!
The Lord of Hosts is with us; The God of
Jacob is our refuge.

JUST ANOTHER CHAPTER 4

Over the past few years, there has been so much talk about our "Founding Fathers." What do we know about them? How about Honest Abe Lincoln? Although not an original founder, but four scores and seven years, after the Declaration of Independence was signed, he spoke at Gettysburg to honor the soldiers who lost their lives in the hope that all people would be equal and free!

Oh, yes! The Gettysburg Address change the scores and the years, and I can hear President Lincoln echoing the same words today:

> Now we are engaged in a great Civil War, testing whether this nation, conceived in liberty and dedicated to the proposition that all mankind is created equal, can long endure?

Can we? Will we?

I've seen portraits of our first president, George Washington, and our sixteenth president, Abraham Lincoln, praying. Our first, who inherited slaves at a young age and obviously didn't know any better (but that's another story), and the other, who said, "Let slavery come to an end!"

In both paintings, they were both bowed down, on their knees. For what and to whom were they speaking?

"I'd like to think" they were talking to that One God, Who rules over our nation—the God and Father of Jesus! I'd also like to think they had a similar prayer to what Jesus prayed just before His crucifixion. "Not my will be done, but Your will be done!

"I'd also like to think" that yes, these "white men," "who brought forth on this continent a new nation," were in one way or another getting their marching orders from God Himself. The same God Whose name appears in our Constitution, our Bill of Rights, our money that states, "In God We Trust," and the same God Whose name President Lincoln spoke about in his Gettysburg Address.

If alive today, I'd like to think he would inspire and encourage us with those very same words: "That this nation, under God, shall have a new birth of freedom, and that this government of the people, by the people, and for the people, shall not perish from the earth."

America has learned much of our people's frustration in the last few years. Perhaps now, God will grant us all a new birth of freedom! A spiritual birth, where Americans, Christians, and Christians from all over the world will pray for God's will to be done here in America.

You see, it's not just these unique men we honor, but we honor our God, to Whom they prayed. We are far from perfect as a people and have misstepped at times as a nation. But I think we can learn a lot from these two portraits, and we can all learn from leaders who pray!

"The time" for the world to find out what America is all about is upon us. Are we really "one nation under God," or will we fall to one of the *isms*? We are being tested! Were these early leaders of our nation standing on "the Rock," Christ Jesus, or shifting sand when writing America's "founding documents?"

We are also going to learn if the combinations of the thoughts presented in the Constitution by mere men and God's Word from the Bible are the proper instruments to operate a government, as well as provide the basis and the basics for a proper education.

Currently, it seems that no matter the debate, and with almost every vote taken in our land, we are split fifty-fifty. God's perspective is, "A divided nation will surely fall!" (Yes, spoken first from the Bible.) So where do we go from here? I'd like to think that, just like George and Abe, we should all be willing to bow down in prayer!

Father, teach us to pray. Help us by Your grace and mercy to lift You as the only King over America. Yes, presidents will come and go, but it is by Your hand and Yours alone that we exist!

Concerning prayer, let us paraphrase Winston Churchill. We will never give in and never, never, never give up! For we know what and who is the TRUTH. And that TRUTH is a person Who said, "I AM the way, the TRUTH, and the life."

So we will take notice that, in Your time, Your Spirit will come to our neighborhoods. And with that, every person, even those with great wealth, those with prominent titles, and every elected official at all levels of our government will sense that the spirit of prayer has come back to our land!

Some will hear, heed, and obey the TRUTH, and some won't! Some will SEE clearly, and some won't!

Father, You tell us that pride goes before destruction and an arrogant, pompous spirit before the fall. But you also say that before HONOR is humility! So help us HUMBLE ourselves before You in the hope that we can be a nation of LIGHT again as America faces her darkest hour.

We ask all these things as Americans, as Christians, and as one nation under God, remembering that it is always dark before dawn! In Jesus's Name! Amen and Amen!

JUST ANOTHER CHAPTER 5

Through prayer and the privilege of voting, may we allow God Himself to do America's "housecleaning!" Too many times, we are hearing of scandals, lies, and misrepresentations in our government, both state and federal.

From the news we see, read, and hear, there are many unsavory culprits from both the Democratic and Republican Parties. There are those today who sit in the seats of governmental authority who know they are guilty of wrongdoings concerning America and feel privileged to take advantage of their titles.

However, if and when God's Spirit comes to our land, "dirty deeds" will be revealed! For God is the great revelator—the one who reveals the truth!

Again, if and when the Spirit of God begins to sweep across America, He will first shake the foundations of all "the little churches," because God's cleansing always starts with God's people! In fact, in time, church denominations will be no more. The fractured body of Christ will be of one mind, one accord—one spirit.

For those who believe in the name of Christ will be called and known simply as "Christians!" And as Christians—temples of God—be sure your lamps are filled with oil, for the days of the "mark of the beast" seem to be quickly approaching!

So let us prepare to put away and hang up our Methodist, Presbyterian, Lutheran, and Catholic denominational garb and so forth, and let the redeemed of the Lord say so!

"I'd like to think" that after "the church's" cleansing, the Spirit will make His way to our nation's capital. Yes, George's City! And just like "the church," He will come like a gentle breeze, a mighty rushing wind, or the earth itself may shake or quake!

Regardless, the job of the Holy Spirit is to always convict and sear consciences. His assignment will be the same as He makes His way through and within the judicial, legislative, and executive branches of the government. And that will include all of our intelligence branches as well.

For those who have taken advantage of their governmental positions of authority, for now, you have beaten the system. For those who have cheated and received much ill-gotten gain with no thought other than to fill their own pocketbooks, for now, you are winning. But before the All-Seeing God comes on to the scene with "great fear" of conviction, you will be well advised to take your "THIRTY PIECES OF SILVER" and go! Go and sin no more!

And to those righteous office holders, drink this in. God has not given you the spirit of fear but of love, of spiritual power, and of God's wisdom—a sound mind. And fear not those who can kill the body. But fear and honor the one Who can kill both body and soul!

Father, for all future candidates, no matter how high or low their position is, please bring to the forefront those who are worthy. Instill in their hearts a willingness to honestly answer the desires of Your heart and aspire to meet the needs of the American people, knowing that, one day, we will all have to answer to You!

Once again, we ask that You do Your perfect work in America. Please allow Your Spirit to go where it may, from family to family, neighborhood to neighborhood, city to city, and state to state, so that the entire world can witness what "one nation under God" looks like!

Not by our own might or by our own power, but by the spirit of prayer, You bless those who call upon Your name! So as Americans and as a Christian nation, we are asking for Your blessings. And in doing so, demonstrate Your awesome power so that Your name may be praised for Your glory!

May it be so! In Jesus's Name!

JUST ANOTHER CHAPTER 6

Maybe now is the time to take a break from American politics and tell you a story! Once upon a time, a man had an affair with his best friend's wife. He was a bachelor, and the friends lived just a short distance from each other. Softball, kegs, grass, and fun were the focus he and his friends shared in the summer of '73.

One night, too much drink and too much smoke brought the two together for a one-night stand. And it only happened once. But the man's conscience gave him no rest afterward. Day and night, he was constantly reminded of what he had done, and he didn't like the feeling.

Playing in as many as three softball leagues, he probably played in more than a hundred softball games that summer. Physically, he was probably in the best shape of his life, but for whatever reason, he found himself wheezing. In time, he could feel what he believed to be a cancer growth in his chest.

A year passed by with a continual feeling of condemnation and guilt. That one-night affair took its toll on him—no peace during the day and no sleep at night.

He had come to his wit's end and decided the best thing for him to do was to kill himself. The guilt ate away at him like cancer, and since he thought he was going to die anyway, what did it matter? He wanted to tell someone, but who? He couldn't tell his best friend and was too embarrassed to tell his mom or dad, even his younger brother, with whom he was very close.

All alone with his thoughts, he pondered suicide. But in his mind, it had to look like an accident so as not to hurt or embarrass his family. A shot to the head, of course, was too obvious, as was hanging or overdosing. How about hitting a tree with his car on a sharp corner of a country road when it's raining?

Perfect! There was a tree that had been hit several times over the years, and it was only four or five miles from his house. Almost eight weeks to the day of his brainstorm—the time was exactly noon—he had just finished lunch, and it started to rain. Talk about your last meal!

Convinced this was the perfect time for his demise, he got into his car and headed toward his final destination. The 97 Rock out of Middletown, New York, was blasting on the radio, but within seconds, the DJ says, "That wraps up our thirty-minute commercial-free rock and roll. Be back soon." He knew "soon" would be about ten minutes, and he had a short trip and wasn't going to hit a tree listening to a commercial.

Back then, you simply turned a knob on the radio to get another station, and a small turn to the right would bring him to WPDH 101.5, in Poughkeepsie, another rock station. But in the middle of the turn, he heard a voice say, "Jesus can save your life." Totally startled, he quickly pulled the car over to the side of the road. He turned the knob frantically back and forth to hear who said that. What religious station was that? But he heard nothing, only silence. For five minutes, he kept going back and forth from one rock station playing rock to the other rock station playing commercials.

Shaking, he turned his car around and headed back home. Running from his car to his bedroom, he fell to his knees and cried, "Jesus, I did something I can't tell anyone else, but I want to tell You!" Releasing all the details of the affair, he asked for forgiveness. Suddenly, in his mind's eye, he saw his past and every sin he had committed, even stealing a couple of soda bottles and a pack of gum when he was a kid.

Upon seeing his sin, he confessed it and asked forgiveness, bawling and squalling, snot flying all over. He got to his feet. He couldn't see, but he could feel and hear that lump of cancer leave his body. Crying even more now, he raised his arms over his head in thanksgiving.

He said, "Jesus, You know I don't read the Bible, and I don't even own a Bible, but I'm going to tell You what I'm going to do. There is this little Presbyterian Church right down the road, and I will go every Sunday."

When his prayer time was over, he looked at his clock. He thought maybe he had been on his knees for fifteen minutes. It was exactly three o'clock. Except for his short ride after leaving his house at noon, he had spent nearly three hours getting all that crap—sin—out of his system and would now breathe without wheezing! And he would never be the same!

Let it be known, I was that man!

Many people, young and old, are committing suicide for many reasons—please stop! If you have nothing to live for, you have nothing to lose by asking Christ into your life! Please take time, even now, to talk to Him, for God is always listening!

May all those who have read this chapter and are contemplating suicide understand that God is waiting for you to give Him your life. And this chapter was meant for you!

JUST ANOTHER CHAPTER 7

Our Dear Heavenly Father,

To You belong all honor, glory, power, and praise! How I wish I had the words to speak to Your heart about our United States of America! Yes, this one nation, we claim, is under Your domain and a pledge of allegiance to this one nation under God—undivided—with liberty and justice for all.

What happened to our belief system in all that? Mere words? Is this what it has come down to, just words with no conviction? Ah, yes, thanks for reminding us. We can't worship two gods at once. Loving one god, we end up hating the other. Adoration of one feeds contempt for the other. We can't serve both God and money!

I guess we have chosen money over You. We have been tempted to chase after the "almighty dollar," and here is where we find ourselves—fighting tooth and nail for position, power, control, titles, prestige—all for the god called money.

Greed has also found a home in our families, our churches, our businesses, the field of entertainment, and almost every level of our government. The devil, with his lies, has presented us with the luscious "apple of greed," and almost all of us, in one form or another, have taken a bite or at least a nibble.

So, Father, we ask You to help turn our lustful, greedy hearts and eyes away from the things of this world and turn our minds toward You. It won't be easy, for Satan is the master manipulator. He shows us the beautiful fruit and elaborate, expensive houses, cars, boats, clothes, shoes, land, and more land, convincing us we can't live without them.

He dulls our senses and confuses our minds with fine wines, various blends of alcohol, and over-the-top drugs. He throws in some pornography, which usually leads to even more bizarre sexual desires, and we find ourselves where we are now—in the dark!

We have been blinded by these temptations, and we now see where they lead us—empty and wanting. The father of lies sucks us into his system of lies and fake promises. Various addictions follow, including entitlement, control, and fame, and now, as a nation, we are caught in his dismal trap of economic, social, and spiritual death!

Recently, the telling of lies has become "an art" here in America. And so much of what we hear and want to believe as truth is nothing more than a product of the enemy's handiwork. Though very few tell the truth anymore, many prefer to hear the lie over the truth. And a lie told over and over again, in time, is believed to be the truth!

Now, You, Lord, tell us that making money and working for better things in life is not a crime, but You also say, "The love for money is the root of all evil. Lust for money brings trouble and nothing but trouble. Going down that path, some lose their footing in the faith completely and live to regret it bitterly ever after."

Father, grant unto us the spirit of prayer so as to clean our hearts and minds. Give us the urgency to pray for our nation's leaders like never before. May Your Holy Spirit now come as a "LAST CALL" for repentance and blow across our land with new clarity, resolve, and love.

Come and bring Your light to a darkened nation that once honored You and You alone. Please give our America another "shot," spiritually speaking. In Jesus's Name!

And all those who love You, say, "Amen!"

JUST ANOTHER CHAPTER 8

When I was growing up in grade school, we sang patriotic songs. One of my favorites was "God Bless America!" I loved the words, and I loved singing it. Over the years, out of nowhere, I would find myself singing it in my car. I started really listening to the words and have concluded we need a rewrite.

Instead of "God Bless America," let's make it "Bless God, America!" and it would go like this:

> Bless God, America, land that we love.
> You stand beside her and guide her
> Through the night with the Light from
> above.
> From the mountains to the prairies
> To the oceans white with foam.
> Bless God, America, for our home sweet
> home.
> Bless God, America, for our home sweet
> home!

How do we bless God? If you read the previous paragraph and had just one thought of "thank you," you are on your way. If we expect to turn our nation around, it starts by giving thanks to our God, repenting of our wrongs, and standing up as a God-fearing people!

Now this is not accomplished in our own strength, for it is God Who is all the while effectively at work in us, energizing and creating in us the power and desire both to will and to work for His good pleasure, satisfaction, and delight.

Father, we love You because You first loved us, and as a nation, we have become like spoiled children. At times, we have fought against You tooth and nail. Too smart, too intellectual, too sophisticated to listen to You anymore.

For the life of me, in 1962, and yet today, I still can't figure out how one woman, Madalyn Murray O'Hair, president and founder of the American Atheists, eventually persuaded our government to take prayers and Bibles out of our schools. How could a supposedly God-fearing country blessed over and over by You let this happen?

How could we even think about taking the Ten Commandments out of our schools, our courtrooms, and many of our government buildings? Just idiotic decisions with disastrous results. We have chased You out and basically turned our backs on You. How foolish!

So over these sixty years, You have gradually left us to our own care. Our TVs, movies, and the news in general show how dark in the heart and mind we have become. Now left in our own filth, COVID-19 comes along, and fear grips our nation. Wringing hands, worried minds, and still many hoping to find salvation through the "mighty dollar."

No dollars or silver, not even gold, can save us from Your discipline. You have told us before that those whom You love, You do discipline. That is also true of a country that claims to be a Christian nation!

Father, as individuals and as a nation, we confess our bad behavior before You and ask for Your forgiveness. We deserve whatever chastening You see fit, for, in the end, it will be for our benefit.

For You say that no discipline is joyful for the present but painful; nevertheless, afterward, it yields the peaceful fruit of righteousness to those who have a relationship with You!

Have mercy upon us, Father. Please restore to us that right relationship with You as Americans, as Christians, and as a nation, and we ask these things in Jesus's Name! Amen and Amen!

Let us bless God, America!

JUST ANOTHER CHAPTER 9

Why would anyone want to write a book? Aren't they taking a great risk of embarrassment and ridicule? Especially if the only people who buy the book are friends and relatives, and chances are very good, they won't read it or like it if they do. Yes, that would hurt!

But wow, there's a lot of people writing them! And I'd like to say it's not easy! Someone once said about doing anything. Be candid about your motives and goals, because authenticity can be the best compass to happiness.

So maybe deep down inside, people write books with the motive and goal of pleasing themselves. "I'm doing this for me!" I want to be recognized! I want to make lots of money! I want to go on book tours! Give me some cameras to watch me! Stick a mic in my face so I might speak! Shouldn't that be my motive, my goal?

Here in America, we are motivated and goal oriented to have the spotlight shine on us! It's the American way! Even if it's just fifteen minutes! I think they call it *fame*!

Fame—that's a funny word! What does that look like? Ever have any *fame*? Again, what does it look like?

I've had some! It always went to my head, thinking I was "something on a stick!" And fame, as quickly as it comes, can go! And when fame is gone, it hits you like a brick. What happened? Just yesterday, I was being applauded, and today, I'm just another face in the crowd!

It seems to me that with "fame" comes privilege, and sometimes, with enough privileges, a dark spirit falls upon the mind and heart. Some may call it "a god complex!" And what is a god complex, you may ask? One definition I found read, "An unshakeable belief, characterized by consistently inflated feelings of personal ability, privilege, or infallibility."

These types of people may even refuse to admit the possibility of their error or failure, even in the face of irrefutable evidence. They may also exhibit no regard for the conventions and demands of society. The word *narcissist* comes to mind. Do you see any such actions in the world today?

Many dictators, so-called kings, emperors, even right down to local politicians, might be carrying a "god complex." And let's face it, it could fall on anyone! Receive enough applause, have people tell you how great you are, win an election, have money thrown at you hand over fist, and see how easily the bait is set for one of the devil's most evil and darkest traps. Hey, and in time, a once-small appetite for fame could grow into a 24-7 craving! And again, it can happen to anyone!

Now some can accept their fall from grace, while some NEVER! And with that, some go into deep depression, and some commit suicide. And then there are others who become angry, bitter, and quarrelsome—perhaps even a warmonger!

So where do you think all these appalling wars and quarrels come from? From the Message Bible,

> They come about because you want your own way, and fight for it deep inside yourselves. You lust for what you don't have and are willing to kill to get it. You want what isn't yours and will risk violence to get your hands on it.

The words that we write and speak may seem of no account, but they can accomplish nearly anything and, for that matter, destroy anything! Remember that it only takes a spark to set off a fire. A careless or wrongly placed word out of a mouth can do that. Through our speech, we can ruin the world, turn harmony into chaos, throw mud on a reputation, send the whole world up in smoke, and go up in smoke with it. Smoke right from the pit of hell!

Father, if we are to receive any so-called fame or glory, let it come from You, and may we thank You for it and, in return, give all the glory back to You! And let us remember not to think more highly of ourselves than we should, for You are still "the all-Knowing God!" And all words and decisions made either by the very rich and powerful or by the very lowly will eventually have to answer to You!

We pray for our government officials, from the president of the United States to our small-town mayors and everyone in between. Please grant them Your wisdom in the hopes of restoring our nation! In Jesus's Name. Amen and Amen!

JUST ANOTHER
CHAPTER 10

"He is no fool who *gives* what he cannot keep to *gain* that which he cannot lose." These words were journaled by Jim Elliot, a missionary martyred in Ecuador in 1956.

Jesus said, "For those who find their life will lose it, and they who lose their life for my sake will find it!"

The Message Bible reads this way: "If you don't go all the way with me, through thick and thin, you don't deserve me. If your first concern is to look after yourself, you'll never find yourself. But if you forget about yourself and look to me, you'll find both yourself and me."

These are hard words to take in and understand. The one word that comes to mind is *surrender*. From early western TV shows as a kid, "Put down your gun, give me your money, and get your hands up" is what I remember as my definition of *surrender*!

To be in that position where a gun is pointed at you is a pretty terrifying and dark place to be. But in God's light, it looks entirely different! "Be gone, in Jesus's Name!" will be my spiritual bullet—my defense! Crazy? Maybe.

I picked up a hitchhiker one day who threatened to shoot me! "What if I told you I have a gun and I plan to shoot you?" asked the rider. To that, I replied, "You can put the gun in my face, but only God can allow you to pull the trigger!" The man started to shake and said, "You are crazier than I am!"

Long story short, he gave his life to Christ! He gave me his Florida Department of Corrections card issued when he was released from jail just the day before, which I still have. So twice in one day, "the captive" had been set free! So, Eric R., if you read this book, I hope it finds you free in HIM and living for HIM!

In all battles, those with the greatest weaponry win the war. In the spirit world, "In Jesus's Name" and "By the Blood of Jesus" are all the weapons we need. Nothing else needs to be said. For "by the Blood" and "in Jesus's Name," darkness and demons must flee! For there is no name greater! No lifeblood is more powerful!

Here's a prayer of Jim Elliot's:

> It makes me boil when I think of the power we profess and the utter impotency of our action. Believers who know one-tenth as much as we do, are doing one hundred times more for God, with His blessing and our criticism. If I could write it, preach it, say it, paint it, anything at all, if only God's power would become known among us!

Father, we pray that Your power and Spirit will become known among us. In Hebrew, the word *experience* means "to know." We desire "to know You" intimately and *experience* You like the world has never witnessed before!

As we surrender our will to Yours, please cleanse us from all our sins, our hurts, our pain, our anger, and our sorrows. Let all of our unforgiveness go so deliverance can flow. Set our spirits free, so we may truly worship thee!

Your *perfect will* is for us to love You with all our heart, mind, soul, and strength, as well as to love our neighbors as we love ourselves. And as we surrender, may we hear Your still, small voice and do all that You ask of us in obedience to You and You alone!

In Jesus's Name, we ask all these things! Amen and Amen!

JUST ANOTHER
CHAPTER 11

There is much darkness over our land! Lawlessness fights to have its ugly way. Right is wrong, and wrong is right! Little is considered sacred. Mass shootings are rampant in our schools, malls, nightclubs, and ball fields. Even churches are not spared. Young children are being molested every day by some who say they represent God. Castrations, mutilation, and sex changes are spoken of openly. Even worse, there are little or no penalties. It is no wonder God has left us to our "own wisdom."

But praying has always been America's strength because our God is our strength. What can happen in America if we pray? From the Book of Books, "For the eye has not seen, nor ear heard, nor entered into the heart of a 'nation,' what our God can do, for, in, with, and through a people that love Him and are called according to His purpose!"

No doubt, because of our personal and/or governmental wickedness, evil has found a home here, and all the weapons in the world can't change the human heart. But, Father, Your Spirit can! If we only had the right words! How about we use Your words and the greatest quid pro quo of all time!

If we, Your people who are called by Your name, humble ourselves, pray, seek Your face, and turn from our wicked ways, *then* You say that You will hear us from heaven, and You will forgive us our sins and *heal* our land!

Father, we want You so much to heal our land, whatever that looks like. We know America is not our real home, for heaven awaits us! But "I'd like to think" that with our prayers, You would reignite this nation as a beacon of light, making it better than ever, and not because of any one man or political party, but because a nation of people prayed for *truth*.

I've seen photos of people holding a Bible in one hand and a gun in the other. And the Constitution gives us the right to protect our individual homes and property and our nation as a whole, and I applaud it—but fighting each other? Really?

For what it's worth, I believe the enemy would rather take away our Bibles than our guns because if a nation does not know God's laws, "so-called leaders," in time, will make up their own rules and laws, totally squeezing God out. It sounds like a few *isms* that exist in the world today.

And again, it's great that our Constitution gives us the right to protect our individual homes and property and our nation as a whole, but if revolution is in the air, how about we check in with You first! For what does God's Word say?

From the Book of Books,

> Blessed be the name of God forever.
> For wisdom and might are His! He changes
> the time and the season; He removes and

raises up presidents and so-called kings
and if they are His; provides both intelligence and discernment.

He will also reveal deep secrets to them, for He knows what lies in the darkness, for He is light. Violent political takeovers are for godless nations! But here in America, let us pray for those who should be our limited-term leaders, and may our God have the final vote!

And for those who would attempt to rig an election, beware, for God will be watching, and He can bring more than fear to those who believe there will be no penalties. For where there is darkness, His light will overcome. For where God's Spirit is, darkness and evil must flee!

Father, You are the beginning and end of our faith. Please breathe Your Spirit upon us, for You said in the last days that You would pour out Your Spirit on all flesh. Cleanse us by convicting us of our wrongs, and may Your Holy Spirit penetrate our hearts and minds so as to exchange our hatred for Your love!

Help us remember and pray for our brothers and sisters across the globe who are being persecuted for righteousness' sake. Let them know that—by Your grace and mercy—we will "hold the line" in the hope that this one nation under your domain never reaches the deranged evils of other countries that are persecuting and killing people because of their beliefs.

In the days to come, may we stand astonished at what You are doing in our individual lives, our homes, our communities, and at every level of government. Please allow those of influence, wealth, and high political positions to find themselves entering that small gate and narrow path that few find. For wide is the gate, and broad is the way that leads to destruction, and many will enter through it!

We are counting on You, Father, to save our nation for Your glory! Knowing that one day, the knees of all people, including all dictators, rulers, presidents, and kings everywhere and throughout all of time, will bow, and every tongue will confess that Jesus, the Christ, is forever Lord and King!

We ask all these things as Americans, as Christians, and as one nation under God! In Jesus's Name! Amen and Amen!

JUST ANOTHER
CHAPTER 12

A short time ago, my daughter and granddaughter visited Rome. While they were there, I asked them if they could find a broken piece from the Roman Colosseum for me. My daughter asked me why. I told her, "In my mind, I look upon the Colosseum as a sacred place because it was there that the powers that be sent our early brothers and sisters to be killed for their belief in Jesus's resurrection."

Initially, Christians were simply run down and run over with horses and chariots. But that was not entertaining enough for the powers that be, so in their intimate wisdom, they brought in lions that would tear them from limb to limb and then devour them. Again, their crime—they wouldn't denounce or deny their faith in Christ.

The Bible tells us that these martyrs—those who were fed to the lions, those who were crucified, those who were stoned to death, these great patriarchs of faith—are cheering us on from on high. Even today!

Now what would they be cheering and shouting from heaven to us? No doubt, they would be quoting scripture: "Lay aside every weight, carry no extra spiritual fat, no parasitic sins, and keep running in the race, yet all the while keeping your eyes on Jesus, the author and finisher of your faith."

They would also be telling us to study how our Lord did it. Why? Because He never lost sight of what His Heavenly Father wanted. He would and could put up with anything along the way, even the despised shame of the cross.

Now faith is the firm foundation under everything that makes life worth living. It is our handle on what we can't see, and these acts of faith are what distinguish our ancestors and set them above and apart from the crowd.

Yes, we will pray for one another, but help us, Lord, to grab hold, embrace, understand, and be motivated by the fact that these same pioneers who stood firm and blazed the way for us two thousand years ago are still up above, encouraging us on.

Father, set us apart from the crowd in the hopes that You will make the United States a great nation of faith once again! Arise in us and quicken us by your Holy Spirit. Let not our souls ever be cast down, but let us find joy unspeakable and full of glory, knowing that You are caring for us in every situation. For our hope is in You, to guide us as individuals and as a nation.

And just like those who gave their lives in Rome, as well as those who are being slaughtered around the world today, we give You ourselves also. Yes, our very lives, to do what You will. For to whom You have set free is truly free, indeed. For we know that heaven is truly our home!

In Jesus's Name! Amen and Amen!

JUST ANOTHER
CHAPTER 13

"Walk a Mile in My Shoes" is a song from the '60s but has been resurrected and is being sung and heard across America once again. Here's a verse or two:

> If I could be you, if you could be me
> For just one hour
> If we could find a way
> To get inside each other's mind,
> Walk a mile in my shoes
> Just walk a mile in my shoes
> And before you abuse, criticize, and accuse
> Just walk a mile in my shoes

Now the song was written by Joe South and sung by many. Even Elvis sang it. But I can hear Jesus saying it.

> If I could be you, if you could be Me
> For just one hour
> If we could find a way
> To get inside each other's mind
> If you could see through My eyes
> Instead of your ego

I believe you'd be
Surprised to see
That you've been blind
Walk a mile in My shoes
Just walk a mile in My shoes
And before you abuse, criticize, and accuse
Just walk a mile in My shoes

Now I wonder where Joe South's head was when he wrote this song. Perhaps when Elvis sang it, he was thinking while singing, *See what money and fame did to me!* Basically, it left me for dead! A prisoner in my own home.

All the money and all the fame never really satisfied "the king," yet that's the very road the world wants us to travel. Get on the fast track, get on the "Train to Fame." "ALL ABOARD!"

So now I'm thinking, *What would it be like to walk in Jesus's sandals—to walk in HIS shoes?* We'd be led by our Heavenly Father, our spiritual hands in His! Hands that bring life to the dead. Hands that heal the deaf, the speechless, and the blind. Even lepers rejoiced when we would come to town.

We'd be speaking words from heaven—words that would make most people ask and say, "From where do these people come from? For no one has ever spoken such words!"

We'd be saying things like, "The perfect will of God is to love the Lord with all your heart, mind, body, and soul!" We'd be answering questions like, "How many times should I forgive my brother, seven?" Seventy times seven would be our reply.

Give us a few biscuits and a couple of fish, along with our Father's blessing, and we're feeding thousands. While fishing, we'd be stopping a storm for our friends with two words: "Be still!"

Perhaps some will think of us as crazy when we tell them, "This world is not our home or kingdom, for our kingdom is to come!" Walking down many roads, many sins will be forgiven, and healing of all sorts will occur— even raising the dead to life!

We are hanging out with the down and out, and that will bother some people who will shout abuse and accusations. Yes, it's those "religious leaders" again, saying, "How is it that you eat and drink with prostitutes, drunkards, tax collectors, and every other kind of sinner?" Our reply will be, "Those who are well have no need for a doctor, but those who are sick do!"

For we did not come to call those "who have it all together" but those who are gripped with sin, and by asking our Heavenly Father for forgiveness, they will be forgiven. They will be shown mercy and live forever because they asked in Jesus's Name!

Now those are some "shoes to walk in!" Grant us those same shoes, Father. In Jesus's Name!

JUST ANOTHER
CHAPTER 14

In my opinion, the three greatest things that can happen in a person's life are finding Christ as one's Savior, being a part of the Lord's return, and hearing a word from God in due season.

From the Book of Books, Psalm 37:25 (NKJV) says, "I was young and now I'm old, yet I have never seen the righteous forsaken or their children begging for bread." It's a beautiful promise and very appropriate for the times—in due season. So how do we get a word from God?

First of all, if it's a word from God, all believers will hear it. The answer will usually come from God's Word—the Bible. And please note that praying is actually a two-way street. "Hearing from God is the other side of prayer!"

Now our Father is not particularly impressed with how much we read, but it's about finding that place in His Word where a particular scripture touches our heart and mind—where the words pop off the page! The words just seem to be enlarged. There's a word for it, but it escapes me now.

But it is a word that applies to us personally upon reading it. And it touches us in such a way that we *know* it's from Him! That verse, that chapter, that book can change a life because God's Word is *living*! So do you understand?

Hearing from God is the other side of prayer. The hearing can come from anywhere or anybody, but whatever we hear, it must line up with the Word of God!

With the Bible in hand, we can ask God to give us a word, our daily bread, so to speak. Try to find that quiet place and sit, kneel, or stand. It's not our body position that God is concerned about, but the position and condition of our hearts.

And know this: He desires an intimate relationship with each one of us. The question is, Do we desire the same? Because we are in a battle, and as good soldiers, this is the time to earnestly seek the Lord while He may be found.

Father, Your love for us is great. You want to do for us more than we could ever dare ask or think. Please help us understand that You are beginning to build up Your body—the church! Christ being the head and we as Your people make up that body.

As You gradually build us up, continue to give us the spiritual muscle to defeat the devil and all the darkness he represents. May Your words be our weaponry and defense!

As Your children, please whisper in our ears a verse or chapter, even a particular book, for us to read from Your Word that touches us, as only You can! In doing so, may those words—Your words—draw us closer to You. For it is written, "You will find me if you search for me with all your heart."

In a letter to the Romans, the apostle Paul writes, "First I thank my God through Jesus Christ for you all, that your faith is spoken of throughout the whole world."

May those same words be echoed around the whole world about America.

Father, do a great spiritual work across our land today and every day as we draw closer to You! And as we draw closer to You, I *know* You will draw closer to us!

For Your honor and glory, Father! We pray and ask, in Jesus's Name! Amen and Amen!

JUST ANOTHER
CHAPTER 15

IF ONLY!

On a day of protest back in June of 2020, then-president Trump stood in front of the Parish House of St. John's Episcopal Church in Washington, DC, with a Holy Bible in hand. In time, with his left arm, he raised it high in the air. I waited patiently for him to speak, but not a word was uttered. IF ONLY!

I thought why, and I don't want to be judgmental, but why did he just hold the Bible in the air? Why did he not read a verse or two from the Book of Books?

I do not wish to be disrespectful, but the Bible is not a "good luck" charm that we wave in the air or have in our homes for some kind of protection while it collects dust year after year. In wartime, it has also been known to stop a bullet—saving a life—but its real purpose comes alive when it is read and spoken!

It could have been a "Founding Father's Day" moment if then-president Trump had read just one verse while a nation sat, stood, and waited for him to speak. One simple verse, who knows, could have brought the "fear (respect) of God" back to America. IF ONLY!

There are many verses he could have chosen. "Fear not!" Jesus said more often than anything else. So from 1 Timothy 1:7, Mr. Trump could have read the verse as a prayer.

For You, Father, have not given us—our America, our people—the spirit of fear! But You grant us power—spiritual power! Power that allows us to love even our enemies. And on top of that, You give us sound minds to be able to differentiate between right and wrong, truth from lies, justice from injustice, and light from darkness!

More than ever, our nation needs Your wisdom. We need You to intervene on our nation's behalf. So we cry out to You as a Christian nation in the hope that "Your will and Your work" will be done on earth as it is in heaven. Help the United States to once again, in our prayers, be grateful for all you do for us!

Preserve our Constitution if it is just! Preserve our Bill of Rights if it is for all people! Grant us a government that serves Your purposes and, most importantly, representatives with hearts and minds for You and our people.

Please make us a praying nation once again. For if we neglect our duty to pray in this hour, America no longer has the right to call itself "one nation under God!"

We wait on You, Father, to do Your work by means of the Holy Spirit!

In Jesus's Name! Amen! IF ONLY!

JUST ANOTHER CHAPTER 16

An Editorial: If I Were Donald Trump's Campaign Manager

I remember during the 2016 presidential debates when Donald Trump was asked a question about forgiveness. His response was, "I can't remember the last time I told someone I'm sorry." *Wow*, I thought, *that's quite the statement!* I'm trying to be a good Christian, and I pretty much say, "I'm sorry," every day, at least to God.

If you, Mr. Trump, plan on serving a second term as president and if "I were your campaign manager," I would advise you to go on a "Forgive-Me Tour."

Instead of insulting those you deem your enemies, why not take a verse or two from the Book of Books—the Bible? Forgive and pray for your enemies, and in your prayer, you might just find that you will need to use the words, "I'm sorry!"

About what, you may ask? Well, it's not my job to judge, so I will leave that between you and the Lord. But a sincere apology, even for name-calling, could soften the hearts and minds of many haters. I know this may be a hard pill for you to swallow, but asking forgiveness can go a long way with God and people.

Let's face it. Those who love you love you! Those who hate you hate you! With these two words, "I'm sorry," you can change some of that.

If, in fact, you are a born-again Christian, is it not your obligation to ask for forgiveness? Just as Christ has forgiven you? And if you forget to whom forgiveness is due, God will reveal it to you. Forgiveness, if you have been forgiven, is a biblical truth and command!

Your campaign slogan will need a slight adjustment: "God Makes America Great!"

If Jesus is your savior, you may want to consider it! Truly, you must know you are not just fighting worldly legal battles but a spiritual war! And the enemy is trying to wear you down daily. If you plan to defeat the enemy on all fronts, you are going to have to trust God to make America great again. And say so!

God Makes America Great! "GMAG!" Put that on your posters, shirts, and hats! What better, and who would want to argue with that? Please step forward!

Now in my humble opinion, when it comes right down to taking care of America's business, you did. I think you did a spectacular job while in office! And you should be commended!

Ah, but if you want to be president once again, the words "I'm sorry" need to be part of your platform. I would add a prayer for America as part of your messaging as well.

I believe that's what Washington and Lincoln would do, unashamedly, during these difficult times.

And instead of threatening your political opponents, remember, "'Vengeance is mine' says the Lord!" Ignore the libel and the slander, and let God and your lawyers do what needs to be done. You continue to convey your plans to the American people and stay the course. Rest in the Lord, and let Him guide you. "Though I walk through the valley of the shadow of death."

If meant sincerely, a "Forgive-Me Tour" would be more than an eye-opener! It would be like "the shot heard 'round the world!" The first time those words were spoken, it was about "a revolution!" For if your campaign is of God, those same words will be used as "a revelation!"

While in office, I thought you and Mr. Mike Pence played well together. Campaigning together in 2016, Pence often quoted scripture from 2 Chronicles 7:14, which, in my opinion, is the greatest quid pro quo of all time.

> *If* and *then*. *If* my people who are called by name will humble themselves, pray, seek my face, and turn from their wicked ways, *then* I will hear from heaven, forgive their sins, and heal their land!

Currently, I know you are at odds with one another; however, maybe it's time for the two of you to get together, iron out your differences, and yes, pray together.

How about some clean, clear, fresh air? I'm not saying Pence should be your running mate, but how about showing the world, as well as your enemies, an honest example of what Christianity is all about—forgiveness! Isn't that what America is all about—preserving the name of Christ? For He is The Greatest Forgiver of all and for all!

Think about it. If your political opponents who at times have shown they despise one another yet can compromise their differences and work together, surely two who say they are Christians can. You both need to understand that where there is no forgiveness, your prayers cannot touch the ears of God. You pray in vain.

Back in the '90s, Christians wore bracelets with the letters WWJD on them. Remember it? It was a reminder to ask themselves, in all situations, "What Would Jesus Do? I will leave it at that.

If we, the people of The United States, are to survive as "One Nation Under God," it is time not just for our leaders but for all of us, as Americans and as Christians, to examine our motives. It's time we make things right with God. And in so doing, seek His wisdom through prayer and by reading His Word, so that, in time, we will receive more of God's Holy Spirit!

So, Father, as Americans and as a Christian nation, we ask that You save *us* from ourselves! Bring *us* back to honoring You as our God. Let the world know—no one man or woman rules America! And without You Father, there is no America! For we are a government of, by, and for the people. And You are our King, our High Ruler, and our Prince of Peace. And Your eyes are always upon *us*!

Whatever plans our enemies may have in store—whether from within or from without—if it be for evil, may You reveal to them that they will not only be fighting *us* but they will also be fighting against You, "the Lord God Almighty." For it is You Who proclaims that darkness will never overtake The Light! And that heaven and earth will pass away, but Your Word—NEVER!

Thank You, Father, for loving us as individuals and as a nation. In Jesus's Name!

Oh! And one last thing, Mr. Trump. Proverbs 16:18 says, "Pride goes before destruction, and a haughty spirit before a fall." But remember Proverbs 15:33, too, "*Humility* comes before *honor!*" I pray you hear His "still, small voice!"

JUST ANOTHER
CHAPTER 17

"Give us this day, Your Word, our daily bread, and forgive us our sins as we forgive those who sin against us" are words from the Bible, known as the Lord's Prayer. It is probably the most spoken and read prayer in America. The words that follow are, "And lead us not into temptation, but deliver us from evil."

Deliver us from evil! For every time an individual or a nation submits to temptation, evil follows. And the great tempter through the years has sashayed his way through our once-humble, God-fearing nation.

Seeking religious freedom, pilgrims came by boats praying and, upon arrival, dedicated this land to Christ in the hope that God's Spirit would always remain here. Now it's a fact that no other nation in the world has proclaimed the Gospel of Christ more than America.

For decades upon decades, no nation has provided more Bibles, gospel tracks, radio and TV programs, missionary workers, money, and relief to the world while asking for nothing but God's blessings in return. And there is no doubt that, since America's birth, God has blessed us because of it.

Perhaps because of it, we've always counted on God to provide ideal weather, ideas that continue to make our lives easier, bumper crops for harvest, cattle for meat, buildings of great architecture, advances in highway and bridge construction, breakthroughs in medicine and science, cars, churches, and, more importantly—freedom. But one day, the tempter came to town, planting in the hearts and minds of the American people the seeds of greed.

As these seeds of greedy thoughts entered our nation's minds, instead of dismissing them, we entertained, watered, nourished, and watched them blossom into full-grown evil. And what is required to satisfy this "need for greed?" Perhaps hiding the truth, lying, cheating, stealing, threatening, or even murder may be required to obtain and to satisfy this new god—*greed*—for the "almighty dollar."

In almost every walk of life, including some church pulpits, we are crying out for money more than God! Even Hollywood tells us, "Greed is good." Ask Gordon Gekko from the movie *Wall Street*. So we are not just turning our backs on God; we are forgetting or just have not been taught that greed, according to the Bible, is one of God's "seven deadly sins."

No wonder some people want the Ten Commandments out of their eyesight and far from their hearing. True greed from an individual, a business, or at any level of government would, no doubt, force them to break as many as half of those commandments. And though we are just looking at one form of evil—temptation—from it, many more evils come along for the ride.

Yet the real pity of it all is that, to some degree, all of us—rich or poor, with no color discrimination, young and old, educated or illiterate—have taken a bite from this forbidden fruit, *greed*. And it has rotted much of our moral standards and pure thought. So from our early years, as a nation serving "the living God," we have turned to the "paper god," money, and are reaping what we have sown.

Deliver us from evil, Father, by Your Spirit. Eradicate all the evil works of the devil from our hearts and minds. From the very weak to those in high positions of power, help us make things right with You.

And though not all will heed, for those who do, make us revelators of Your Word and keep us in serious pursuit of You in our prayers, thoughts, and deeds.

May our weapons of warfare against the devil be weapons of prayer and mighty in You in bringing down the stronghold of greed. Chase the darkness from every state within the boundaries of our nation, for we know the darkness of evil cannot withstand Your holy light—the light of the Spirit.

We are asking You to deliver us with "one last call" of repentance and righteousness. Grant to America the spirit of prayer, and by Your hand, remold and remake this divided and broken nation once again as a beacon of light for all the world to see! Make us "one nation under God, undivided, with liberty and justice for all."

In Jesus's Name, we pray, Father!

JUST ANOTHER
CHAPTER 18

I want to tell you a story!

It's about a time in my life, a couple of years after a divorce and coming to Siesta Key, Florida. I was just hired by a Sarasota radio station, WISP 98.7 FM. It has since moved to Tampa, but back in 1992, it was a brand-new station, and they brought me there from New Jersey to expedite revenue through sales and marketing—advertising.

At this time, I was basically running from lost love and God. Even worse, I believed God couldn't love me anymore because of the divorce. To make a long story short, just starting a new job, paying child support, and trying to keep my own head above water proved to be strenuous and difficult!

Spending fifty to sixty hours a week making phone calls, "cold-calling" up and down city streets and county roads for the radio station, and becoming a weekend bouncer at the Beach Club kept me plenty busy and tired. Things were so tough that when the secretary from the station would "beep" me to call into the office, I had to tell her, "Don't bother beeping me because I don't have a quarter for the phone booth!"

Now the money I was making allowed me to cover my overall expenses, but I was left with very little for food. My diet for three consecutive months consisted of bread, eggs, and potatoes, except on Sunday. Ah, Sundays! My "gourmet meal"—one hot dog on a piece of bread with mustard! My treat for the week!

So nearing the end of these three long months and after an exhausting week, Sunday finally came. I went to the freezer where I kept my package of "tube steaks" and discovered there was not one to be found! To this day, I'm not sure what happened to that dog. Maybe I did eat the last one late one night, or I simply forgot to buy a new eight-pack; regardless, it was a tough pill to swallow!

So trying to stay positive, I thought to myself, *I will pretend there is a hot dog on my bread and spread the mustard on thick.* As I went to grab my "loaf" of bread, I noticed that only the end slice was there—the heel—and only three-quarters of that. Still trying to remain positive, I got my mustard jar from the refrigerator, only to find it would take a spoon and about three minutes to scrape out enough mustard to lightly cover the heel of bread and my "imaginary" hot dog!

Hungry, angry, and totally losing it, I started ranting and yelling at God! "I can't believe You are treating me like this, and I'm sick of it!"

Then He spoke back, in His still, small voice, "You have so much more than the rest of the world!"

I immediately dove prostrate on the kitchen floor!

Shaking all over yet not making a sound, I heard, "You have running water, a toilet, a roof over your head, air-conditioning, clean clothes, a car..." and then he stopped talking. With my eyes closed, He let me see some of the poverty in the world. Mud huts, no plumbing, people gathering water with buckets, children with dirty, ragged clothes, starvation, and babies with swollen bellies. And the more I saw, the more I cried. And with that, I cried out, "I don't want to see anymore! I will be content with what I have and will never complain to You again!"

Of course, before I got to my feet, I realized how blessed I really was, and from there, I began to be very thankful for what I had. I've always loved my country, but on that day, I learned to appreciate it even more.

Maybe I wasn't eating caviar and thick steaks with a fine glass of wine, but I had more—a lot more than the rest of the world. For I found that, for so many people around the world, even a three-quarter piece of bread with a little mustard would be considered "a gourmet meal!"

America is a blessed nation, and if our country's citizens would visit, for just a day, some of the remote parts of the world, they would kiss this ground upon return!

Sometime after that "experience," I spent some time in some remote areas of India. Some people were living in mud huts, with chickens running in and out. There was no electricity, no phones, and no shoes for the children. They have worn-out clothes and four or five different ponds of water: one for drinking, one for washing clothes, one for bathing, and one representing the "outhouse."

So after some time with my newly found brothers and sisters, I asked through an interpreter if they were angry at

God for them being born in India. The interpreter's reply was no, but he added, "It could be worse!"

My immediate question was, "What could be worse?" The response, again through the interpreter, was, "We could have been born in Africa."

So I asked, "What was the difference?"

The response was, "We have water!"

Wow! Here were people who were thanking God for the monsoon season—four to six months of rain, while the rest of the year is nothing but hot, hot, hot! Needless to say, I had a newfound love for my new Christian brothers and sisters and even a greater appreciation for America!

The apostle Paul wrote,

> I have learned the secret of living in every situation, whether it is with a full stomach or empty, with plenty or with little. For I can do all things through Christ who strengthens me!

Father, as Americans and as Christians, may we become content and more thankful for all You give us here in America! We trust in You and You alone! Our faith is in You and You alone! Please watch over us as darkness tries to extinguish the freedom You have given us! Make us once again people of prayer, and in doing so, I know we will become richer for it as individuals, as part of Your church family, and as "one nation under God!"

For You have told us, Father, "Eye has not seen, nor ear heard, nor has entered into the heart, the things God has prepared for those who love You and are called according to Your purpose."

Help us be strong in You, Father! In Jesus's Name! Amen and Amen!

JUST ANOTHER
CHAPTER 19

Of the many movies I've seen, *Cinderella Man* has always been one of my favorites! It's a true story about a boxer from Hoboken, New Jersey. Jim Braddock was his name, and early in his career, he was a serious contender as "Heavyweight Champion of the World."

He broke his right hand a couple of times, and instead of letting it heal, he kept fighting. Soon, his age and some nagging injuries caught up to him. Simply put, his boxing days were over! Actually, he was forced to quit. The boxing commission took away his license to box. That's how bad of a fighter he had become.

"The Great Depression" followed his losing streak, and with a family of five, he looked for work on the docks. If chosen to work from the multitude seeking the few daily vacancies, he was picked sparingly, and if chosen, he'd be working all day for five dollars a day.

A year went by, and he and his family were struggling, with little food and no money for electricity—desperate times! But because of a prebout injury, Braddock's old manager asked him if he would fight this ex-marine by the name of John "Corn" Griffin.

Now Griffin was in line to fight the reigning champion Max Baer, but because Griffin's challenger got injured so close to fight night, Madison Square Garden as well as the boxing commission needed someone, anyone, who was willing to fill in. It would be a "one-time" shot for Braddock. So of course, for a purse of two hundred dollars, Braddock was more than willing to jump into the ring! Being out of the ring and having no training for well over a year, it was basically a suicide mission!

Surprisingly, however, Braddock beat Griffin by a technical knockout! Braddock had found that he now had a powerful left hand! Working at the docks, he realized his twice-broken right hand was basically useless, so he had to compensate by depending on his left. Little did he know that this practice would turn the tide in his favor.

Early on, it was deemed that this would be "the only" fight he would get; however, because of his victory, his manager convinced the boxing commissioner to reinstate him, thus giving him an opportunity to fight one more time.

With Griffin "knocked out" of contention, Braddock's next fight would be against John Henry Lewis, who was now next in line for a shot at the title but needed a warm-up bout before the championship fight.

Now Lewis beat Braddock a few years back and beat him up badly. So of course, all the betting money was on Lewis. But midway through the fight, Lewis came back to his corner after a grueling round and was slumped on his stool. His manager slapped him across the face and said,

"What's wrong with you? You beat this guy to pulp the last time you fought him!"

And this was the line—a line I will never forget! As Lewis looked at his manager, he was peeking across the ring at Braddock, saying, "He ain't the same guy!"

This is what we want the devil to say about us as we embrace our own personal prayer life on behalf of our nation. THESE CHRISTIANS AREN'T THE SAME WORLDLY PEOPLE THEY USED TO BE!

We know we are being "knocked around" a little, Father, but we are not "counted out!" As Christians, as Americans, and as one nation under God, help us "stand up to kneel down" before You daily. For in doing so—out of love—You will strengthen us!

We thank You for preparing us to do battle against the wiles of the devil, pulling down strongholds, casting down arguments, and every high thing that exalts itself against the knowledge of God.

No longer will we be just reading Your Word and seeking Your face for a feel-good moment. But in doing these things, You will be equipping us, building us up in the faith, and giving us spiritual muscle daily to do Your *work*!

For Jesus said, "My Father is always at work!" And we want to "get in the ring" and throw a few knockout punches against the devil's work—with You in our corner, of course!

May it be so! In Jesus's Name! Amen and Amen!

By the way, Braddock did become Heavyweight Champion of the World by defeating the then-reigning champion Max Baer. Great movie!

JUST ANOTHER
CHAPTER 20

I want to tell you another story.

When I became a Christian, I remember talking to the Lord one afternoon about trying to stay away from the influences—of my friends. It's not because they were bad people, but when we got together, it was basically a party with lots of "refreshments!" And oftentimes, I was the entertainment, I'm sorry to say.

So because I didn't want to do the party scene anymore, I asked the Lord, "How am I going to leave friends whom I've known for years? How are they going to understand this? I can't just walk away from them, can I?" By evening, the Lord gave me my answer.

I was listening to Moody Radio, and a preacher—I can't recall his name—was preaching on the new life in Christ that we should be experiencing when, out of nowhere, his message changed gears. He said, "Now for all you new Christians out there who are concerned about losing your friends, don't worry about it! Believe me! You don't have to worry because the more you talk to them about Jesus, they are going to lose you."

I got a couple of laughs out of that. Firstly, because of the way the preacher said it, and I was pretty sure he was right. Secondly, how quickly the Lord answered my prayer and the means by which He did it. Who knew?

It was then that I learned that God can talk to us in any manner He wishes. Reading the Bible is where He speaks to us the most, of course, but there are other means, as I found out early on! But I also learned that whatever we hear or from whomever we hear it, let's make sure it always lines up with the Word of God! And be particularly sure it's not heresy or gossip!

For if we should be in "the last days," the Word says, "In those days there will be many false teachers, preachers, and so-called prophets." So let us verify and test the spirits, and we may even want to get confirmation (hear the same thing two or three times from different sources) for greater assurance.

So from the Message Bible,

> My friends, don't believe everything you hear. Carefully weigh and examine what people tell you. Not everyone who talks about God comes from God. And from the secular world, be careful not to confuse lies with the truth, for there are many lying spirits in the world.

So with that, Father, we know we are to love our enemies and pray for those who wish us ill will, but may we always remember to Whom we belong and Your Word that says to pray for but do not become partners with those who reject God. How can you make a partnership out of right and wrong? That's not a partnership—that's war. Is light best friends with dark? Does Christ go strolling with the devil? Does trust and mistrust hold hands? Who would think of setting up pagan gods in Your Temple? But that is what we are; every believer in Christ, is a temple, in which God's Spirit lives.

God Himself put it this way:

> "I'll live in them, move into them; I'll be their God and they'll be my people. So leave the corruption and the compromise for good," says the Lord. "Don't link up with those who will pollute you. I want you all for myself. I will be a Father to you; and you shall be children to me." (2 Corinthians 6:14–18 MSG)

Therefore, having these promises, beloved, let us make a clean break from everything that defiles or distracts us both from within and without. Let's make our entire lives fit and holy temples for the worship of God!

Father, we will witness to the unbelievers, but in doing so, help us not to become friends with the world! Please lead us always to those who will have ears to hear and need Your help. And please make us not just hearers but also doers of Your Word by Your Spirit!

May we become strong in the Spirit for our own sake, the church's sake, our nation's sake, and all for Your glory! In Jesus's Name, we ask it!

JUST ANOTHER
CHAPTER 21

From the Book of Books—The Bible—the manual for living, and as I like to call it, the "History of the Future," Jesus speaks of a time frame—"a generation"—and this is what the planet will look like.

He said that many false prophets would arise. The world will hear of wars and rumors of wars. Nations will rise against nations. Kingdoms or dictatorships will rise against other dictatorships. There will be famines, pestilence, and earthquakes in various places. Yes, the real climate change!

The apostle Paul adds an even more elaborate detail on what the world will see in that generation. There will be difficult times. People will be self-absorbed, money-hungry, boasters, self-promoting, disobedient to parents, unforgiving, crude, headstrong, slanderers, impulsively wild, cynical, treacherous, ruthless, addicted to lust, and allergic to God.

If we happen to be part of that generation, which is a pretty accurate account of what we see today, perhaps it's time to partner with God on the greatest "quid pro quo" ever known to the human race. So what is a quid pro quo? Simply stated, if you do this for me, I will do this for you.

God's quid pro quo says, "*If* my people, who are called by my name, will humble themselves, pray, seek my face, and turn from their wicked ways, *then* I will hear from heaven, forgive their sins, and heal their land." Yes, I wrote it again!

So where does this bring us? I believe it's our time and season, as individuals, as the body of Christ, and as a nation, to put on the whole armor of God as found in the Bible in Ephesians 6:11.

If we are living in that "generation," please quicken it to our hearts, Lord. For surely, it would be our time and season to pray and to call upon the name of the Lord!

JUST ANOTHER
CHAPTER 22

Recently, many of our city streets have been swarmed with people who have demonstrated a violent dislike for our Founding Fathers. These protesters have even the same disdain for President Abe Lincoln, who, less than ninety years later, wanted no more than to "set the captives free!"

What we currently do know about our country's early leaders is that people have been pulling down their statues in the hopes they can erase their names and images from America's history. We've heard their angry cries and hatred for these "slave-owning tyrants!" Even hatred for the "tyrant" who brought forth the Emancipation Proclamation.

In all fairness, "I'd like to think" that this nation's early leaders were "spirit-filled" men. But with what spirit were they filled? By an evil spirit or by the Holy Spirit? That's the debate, and so for now, we are in a stalemate, and it has reached a plateau.

Perhaps "the hour" to settle this great American debate has come upon us! And that is a good thing! For the hour has certainly presented itself to learn and reveal if America is really "one nation under God" and if there truly is justice for all!

And with that, every American should want to know and needs to know if believing in these "founding documents," written by men, and "the Bible," written by God, in which much wisdom and knowledge were gathered, would and could stand as a proper foundation on which a nation can survive. Are these documents and the Bible solid enough to hold the United States together? That time of judgment has come to America, and I pray we are not found wanting!

One beautiful thing about America is that when the Revolutionary War was won, our first president, George Washington, didn't declare himself *king*! And if the temptation was there, thank God he did not take a bite from that apple!

So now it's "our time" to ask our nation's leaders: From what apple are you munching on? "I'd like to think" that all of our presidents—past, present, and future—would consider God's thoughts and ways before their own wants and desires concerning America.

Perhaps it is time for our leaders and especially all future presidential candidates to think upon the words of John the Baptist, whose ego enabled him to say concerning God, "He [Jesus] must increase, but I must decrease." May they also ponder the words of Jesus Himself, Who prayed, "Father, not my will, but your will, be done!" Now that would be a real revelation!

Honestly, how refreshing it would be for all of our government officials to work together for the betterment of the American people, both rich and poor. And how fair and satisfying it would be for them to receive wisdom, insight, and marching orders from God, Whose name appears in our Constitution, our Bill of Rights, and "In God We Trust," is proudly printed on our money and the same God Whom President Lincoln spoke about in his Gettysburg Address!

Perhaps these recent protesters who mock America's ideology have a just cause. And there is no doubt there have been many injustices, both in the past and the present. But as God-fearing people and by way of our First Amendment rights, we have the freedom to pray, and in time, God can make things right—for all!

However, if these "Americans," who cannot and will not see past their hatred for what America supposedly stands for and who want nothing to do with our God, BEWARE. For God says in His Word that those who avoid and distrust Him are in the dark and don't see life. All they experience of God is darkness, and an angry darkness at that!

Here are the facts from God's perspective: A divided nation will surely fall! So the question is, Is God in our land? Another is, Will the foundation of this American ideology that was built on faith and prayer withstand this hour of darkness?

Most, if not all, Americans, as well as much of the world, know that America, like the *Titanic*, looks to be sinking. And soon, the world is about to find out if America's foundation was built on sinking sand or on the rock—Christ Jesus!

JUST ANOTHER
CHAPTER 23

Did you ever work hard on something, only to have that dream just go up in smoke? All your time, energy, and effort were wasted. It's frustrating! That's happening here in America more than ever before.

From two different interpretations of the New King's James Bible and the Message Bible, I read Luke 6:20–28,

> KJV
>
> Blessed are the poor, for yours is the kingdom of God.

> Message
>
> You're blessed when you've lost it all. God's Kingdom is there for the finding.

> KJV
>
> Blessed are you who hunger now, for you shall be filled.

Message

You're blessed when you are ravenously hungry. Then you're ready for the Messianic meal.

KJV

Blessed are you who weep now, for you shall laugh.

Message

You're blessed when the tears flow freely. Joy comes with the morning.

KJV

Blessed are you when men hate you, and when they exclude you, and revile you, and cast out your name as evil, for the Son Of God's sake. Rejoice on that day, and leap for joy! For indeed your reward is great in Heaven. For in like manner their fathers did to the prophets.

Message

Count yourself blessed every time someone cuts you down or throws you out, every time someone smears or blackens your name to discredit God. What it means is that the truth is too close for comfort and that person is uncomfortable. You can be glad when that happens—skip like a lamb, if you like—for even though they don't like it, I DO says The Lord… and all Heaven applauds. And know that you are in good company; my preachers, my witnesses, my children have always been treated like this.

KJV

But woe to you who are rich, for you have received your consolation.

Message

But it's trouble ahead if you think you have it made. What you have is all you get.

KJV

Woe to you who are full, for you shall hunger.

Message

And there's trouble ahead if you are satisfied with yourself. Your SELF will not satisfy you for long.

KJV

Woe to you who laugh now, for you shall mourn and weep.

Message

And there's trouble ahead if you think life's all fun and games. There's suffering to be met, and you're going to meet it.

KJV

Woe to you when all men speak well of you, for so did their fathers to the false prophets.

Message

There's trouble ahead when you live only for the approval of others, saying what flatters them, doing what indulges them. Popularity contests are not truth contests. Your task is to be true, not popular.

One more, last one!

KJV

But I say to you who hear; love your enemies, do good to those who hate you, bless those who curse you, and pray for those who spitefully use you.

Message

To you who are ready for the truth, I say this; love your enemies. Let them bring out the best in you, not the worst. When someone gives you a hard time, respond

with prayer for that person. And pray IN
JESUS'S NAME!

Father, only through Your Holy Spirit can we lead
such a life as this, so if You would, fill US to overflowing
and give US the mind of Christ that we, who have ears to
hear, honor these words in our character. In Jesus's Name!
Amen and Amen!

JUST ANOTHER
CHAPTER 24

Father, can we sit at Your feet for a while and reason together?

You said in Your Word that You would search our hearts and examine our minds to get to the root of who we really are and define our purpose. You convict us, and we are always better for it. For who knows us better than You? For there is no hiding from You, no pretense! David was a man after Your own heart, You have told us, and though he sinned many times, he was still a man after Your own heart. Why?

Simply stated, "I'd like to think" that once he was convicted of his sins, his wrongdoings, he quickly asked for forgiveness and said, "Against You and You alone have I sinned!" Why should we not be of the same character?

In Psalm 51 (NKJV), David, after being found out about his affair with Bathsheba, prayed the following. Let us make it our prayer as well!

> Have mercy upon me Oh God, according to your love and kindness, according to the multitude of your tender mercies. Blot out my bad behavior, wash me thor-

oughly from my iniquity and cleanse me from my sin. For I acknowledge my bad behavior and my sin is always before me. Against You and You alone have I sinned and done this evil in your sight. For I was brought forth in iniquity, and in sin my mother conceived me.

But you desire truth in the inward parts and in the hidden part you will make me know wisdom. Wash me in Your Spirit and I shall be clean. Wash me and I shall be whiter than snow. Hide your face from my sins and take away all my wickedness.

Now adultery may not be the sin that burdens our lives, but whatever our personal sin is, let us pray his words for our America.

Create in us, as Americans and as a Christian nation, a clean heart, O God, and renew a steadfast spirit within us. Do not cast us away as individuals and as a nation from Your presence, and do not take Your Holy Spirit from us. Restore to us the joy of our salvation and uphold us by Your generous Spirit. Then we will teach the lawless Your ways, and sinners will be converted to You!

Let us listen to what the Holy Spirit is saying from the Book of Books:

> "Come now, and let us reason together," says the Lord. "Though your sins be as scarlet, they shall be white as snow; though they be red like crimson, they shall be as pure wool!"

May Your perfect will be done in America, Father! In Jesus's Name. Amen and Amen!

JUST ANOTHER
CHAPTER 25

One day during COVID-19 days, I noticed a neighbor scrubbing the floor of her back porch. I yelled out to her, "How are you today?"

"I'm great now," was her reply. "I've spent all day giving my house a deep cleaning, and I'm just about finished. It was hard work, but it was worth it. The place looks great and smells so clean after being cooped up for so long."

Just the way she so strongly emphasized "a deep cleaning" thoroughly took me by surprise! I was thinking, *My place can use a* DEEP CLEANING! I could tell she was working hard, her hair strown left and right while wiping her forehead with the back of her hand. She looked entirely drained.

I started thinking, *I had never heard of a deep clean before. I mean, I've done some serious cleaning, some good cleaning, even a fine job cleaning, but a deep cleaning? Never!*

The more I thought about it, the more I thought she was cleaning all day. *That must mean she cleaned inside and under the refrigerator, moved chairs, washed windows, dusted, vacuumed under the bed, scrubbed toilets, and more! That is* DEEP! *Now I'm no slob, but if I'm going to move a refrigerator around to clean under it, do the dishes, add a load of laundry, and do a little vacuuming, I consider that a great day of cleaning!*

I then started thinking of the spiritual side of a "DEEP CLEANING," and instead of smelling that "clean scent" of bleach and Windex, as a Christian nation, we should do some deep cleaning in our hearts and minds so as to "clean up" our lives for God and have the "fragrance and aroma" of Christ.

Father, we give You permission. We invite you in to do a deep cleaning of our hearts and minds as individuals and as a nation. We know it's hard to confess and cry out earnestly about all of our individual as well as our national guilt, shame, greed, lust, hurts, sorrow, pain, frustration, weaknesses, compromising attitudes, anger, fears, hatreds, wrongdoings, addictions, lost loves, and broken hearts. Quit the list, but we will give it to You.

"Come and let us reason together," is what You say. "Come unto Me, and I will give you rest!" You also say, "*If* we humble ourselves, pray, and seek Your face, *then* You will hear from heaven, and You will heal our land." Again, the greatest "quid pro quo" of all time!

If we, as Your people, ask forgiveness and give you the honor, respect, and praise you deserve, then You will spare our country and heal our land by Your Holy Spirit. And no force, not even the spirit of the Antichrist, can stop it, nor can a weapon be formed!

So with that, Father, help us do our part. Allow us to bury our pride and give way to Your will in the hope You will do a deep cleaning in our hearts, minds, bodies, and souls! Let us live in, by, for, and through our Savior and Lord Jesus Christ! By doing so, we pray that You and You alone will receive all the glory.

And as we bow down to You, Father, as "one nation under God," we ask that you whisper in our ears the same words You speak to Israel: "You will be my people, and I will be Your God!"

We ask these things in Jesus's Name! Amen and Amen!

NOT JUST ANOTHER
CHAPTER 26

There comes a time in almost everyone's life, if not in all lives, where one asks themselves, "What am I doing? What am I here for? Is this life worth living?

I can profoundly say, "Yes! Life is worth living!" Because this earth may not be your real home. Perhaps you are just passing through? Waiting, as *The Jeffersons* would say, "Movin' on up, moving on up, to that deluxe apartment in the sky."

So if you're reading this and feel that there is no hope, no love to be found, and no escape from a drug, and you're depressed to the point where you are suicidal, take a walk with me. No, not down memory lane, at least not for now, but down a road known as the Roman Road, and the map is found in the Bible.

And I thought that instead of just typing up some scriptures, maybe you and I could pray this prayer together.

Dear God in heaven, I am so glad that you are not a respecter of people. Meaning, neither Jew nor Gentile, whether my color is red, yellow, brown, black, or white, whether rich or poor, and no matter what my condition is, like any good dad, You're there to help me in my hour of need. Today, in this hour, I need You!

I have made so many mistakes, and I can't seem to make them right. I hate myself and the world I live in. I want out! But I'm afraid, Lord. I'm really afraid! Should I just take my life without at least considering You first? I'm at the end of my rope. I need to be saved from myself and from my life's situation.

I've read from Romans chapter 3 that "there is none righteous, no not one!" No person on earth does good, no not one! You add, "For all have sinned and come short of Your glory. So I come to You, admitting, I AM a sinner."

I have also read that if I confess with my mouth the Lord Jesus and believe in my heart that God has raised Him from the dead, and because I am praying, calling out to You, and asking forgiveness, I can be saved! And in believing, I will not be put to shame! Please help me believe that!

Please grant me Your peace, for You say that, by faith, I can be justified and forgiven. So take me down memory lane, Lord. And while on the path, let me see all my wrongs, and as I see them, I will confess them and ask forgiveness for all my sins. Take all the poison from my mind, and by Your Holy Spirit, set me free. For Jesus said, "Who the Son sets free is free indeed!" Thank You, Father, for my new freedom! In Jesus's Name! Amen and Amen!

Now go find a church where Christ is preached, or call one or the many who have tried to talk to you about God over the years. Especially seek out that one or more whom you know has been praying for you, in some cases, for years. For every day that turns, there is a season. I pray that the season of knowing God personally comes today. In Jesus's Name.

If you would like to look up where the Roman Road is in the Bible, check the following: Romans 1:20–21, Romans 3:23, Romans 5:8, Romans 6:23, Romans 8:1, Romans 10:9–10, Romans 10:13, and Romans 11:36.

Be blessed!

JUST ANOTHER
CHAPTER 27

Today, we hear much about inflation. Simply stated, the price of almost anything purchased will rise.

Unfortunately, inflation can lead to a recession—a temporary decline during which trade and industrial activity are slowed—which could then lead to depression.

For a decade, America was entrenched in an economic depression known as the Great Depression. It took its true form when the stock market crashed in October 1929.

If America were to go through a "greater depression," the landscape would look totally different. For back then, for the most part, people still held some moral value, so the "elite," with their money and an array of luxuries, were pretty much left alone and safe.

Today, however, that would be a totally different story. Being seen by some, your jewelry, your car, your boat, and even your private jet could be stolen. Perhaps it can even lead to fatality! Gates, walls, and fences won't be high enough to stop desperate thieves. And beware, you very, very rich, for even your "bodyguards" may turn on you in time! No! Compared to "the thirties," these are totally different times in which we live!

Now I've never stood in a soup line, yet they will exist in large numbers should depression hit. Even worse, in time, if you have money, you may need special identification to make purchases. The identification—a chip with three sets of six numbers (666)—is found under the skin of one's wrist or forehead. It is called "the mark of the beast!"

Wow, take on the *mark*, or your buying days are over! However, let it be known that taking on this identification is a definite "no-no" in the eyes of the Lord. As a matter of fact, God Himself calls it an abomination.

So what should our attitude be, and what would be our thought process should such circumstances arise? FAITH! Faith that our God will be with us!

I'd like to think that I would have the attitude and faith of the prophet Habakkuk (Ha-buh-kuhk), who wrote in his plight:

> Though the fig trees may not blossom, Nor fruit be on the vines; Though the labor of the olive may fail, And the fields yield no food; Though the flock may be cut off from the fold, And there be no herd in the stalls—Yet I will rejoice in The Lord, I will joy in the God of my salvation. (Habakkuk 3:17–19 NKJV)

Now that is a testimony. Famine has engulfed the land, yet he praises his God! Job went even further: "Though He slays me, yet I will trust Him!"

As Christians and as Americans, do we truly trust in our God? For those who do, this is not the time nor the hour to become "Doubting Thomas!"

Ever heard of the story of David and Goliath? When Saul, King of the Jews, saw the teenage boy, David, he said, "You are not able to go against this giant Philistine [believed to be seven feet to ten feet tall], for you are a youth, and he has been a man of war since his youth."

David quickly responded, "Although I am a shepherd, once when a lion and another time when a bear took one of my lambs, I chased them down, and I killed them."

David knew, without a doubt, that God was with him. So with one small stone he let fly from his slingshot, he hit Goliath between the eyes, bringing down the giant and saving his country!

So with many, perhaps a few, or maybe just one person, like David, holding the hand of God, America, too, can be saved. Even Sodom and Gomorrah would have been spared destruction if God had found ten righteous people within their borders. Just ten!

Father, let us take a trip down memory lane as individuals and as a nation. Help us remember all the things You have brought us through in the past and, in doing so, increase our faith and refill us with a fresh and new relationship with Your Holy Spirit. For it seems that our nation is under a spell of unbelief, deceit, and lies. It seems that the spirit of the Antichrist continues to make its way to America and throughout the world.

Please embed in our hearts and minds what the apostle Paul wrote to the Romans: "If God is for us, who can be against us?" He adds,

> No matter what the world throws at us, we are more than conquerors through Christ.
>
> For we believe and are persuaded that neither death, nor life, nor angels, nor principalities, nor powers, nor things present, nor things to come, nor height, nor depth, nor any other created thing shall be able to separate us from the love of God, which is in Christ Jesus our Lord.

Thank You for Your promises, Father, and may Your army of angels protect our boundaries, and may Your Holy Spirit sweep across this "one nation under God," chasing all darkness from Your path. In Jesus's Name! Amen and Amen!

JUST ANOTHER
CHAPTER 28

The thunder roared, the lightning pierced through the darkened sky, and with a loud voice, Jesus cried out, "My God, My God, why have You forsaken me?"

Ever been there? There now? Why did Jesus, the Son of God, cry out such words? It's my understanding because, for the first time, Jesus was not one with His Father. It wasn't the cross that made him cry out, but the fact that He was all alone was the real agony.

Our Father had to turn His back on Him! For at that time, He represented sin, all of humanity's sin, and our Father God cannot look upon sin. Sin separates. So where there is sin, prayers are hindered.

Father, we love You because You first loved us, and You said You would never leave or forsake us, so help us confess our sins, hurts, pain, sorrow, ill will, and hatred toward others, which You say is the same as having a murderous heart. Take it from us!

We are asking for Your deliverance, and though our sins are as scarlet, You can make them as white as snow. In our confession, You said You would remove our sins as far as the East is from the West. Your Word also says You know our frames, and You remember that we are nothing more than dust.

Perhaps it's time and season to bury our laughter and cry about our nation's plight. Perhaps the battle between light and darkness and good and evil and the separation of sheep and goats and wheat and weeds has begun. Today, we call upon Your name, Lord, and pray and seek Your face like never before. People's lives and our nation's life are at stake, both spiritually and physically.

Please save and spare our nation from the various disasters that seem to be all around us. May You start up the wind of Your Holy Spirit from our entire eastern seaboard, across our mountains, prairies, and fruited plains to our western shores, including Alaska and Hawaii. We ask that Your name be glorified and that every nation see and hear what "one nation under God" looks like!

And in so doing, may every leader around the world have a revelation that, one day, every knee will bow and that every tongue will confess that Jesus Christ is King and Lord. We ask this in Jesus's Name! Amen and Amen!

JUST ANOTHER
CHAPTER 29

The foundation for learning in America began with reading the Bible. Yes, reading, writing, and arithmetic were added, but the mainstay of the "system" early on came from "the Book of Books," the Bible.

As the years went by, the arts, history, language, science, economics, and even physical education were added, but the Bible remained in the classroom! In my primary grades, the Bible was still part of the curriculum.

In 1962, that ended, but during those early years, the first thing we would hear every morning after the Pledge of Allegiance would be the teacher reading from the Bible. It was usually about a five- to ten-minute read. There was no preaching. The Bible's chapters and verses are what we heard, with hopes that we were hearing from God.

What did I learn? The same things our kids of today can learn! Basically, how to act!

If one was to read a chapter a day from Proverbs, starting on the first day of the month, that would equate to thirty-one days; they would find a wealth of knowledge, wisdom, and good common sense, and for those without a dad, instructions and insight into how to live an upright and moral life and become a person of good character.

Want a great foundation for a solid education? I challenge anyone who will read Proverbs for twelve consecutive months daily, chapter by chapter, based on the day of the month, not to be richer and wiser in character for doing so!

For example, since today is the 4th of the month, I will read Proverbs chapter 4 (NKJV).

> Hear my children, the instruction of a Father, And give attention to know understanding; For I give good doctrine; Do not forsake my law.
>
> Hear and receive my sayings, And the years of your life will be many. I have taught you in the way of wisdom; I have led you in right paths. When you walk, your steps will not be hindered, And when you run, you will not stumble. Take firm hold of instruction, do not let her go; Keep her, for she is your life. May it be so! In Jesus's Name.

IT IS FINISHED

In the book *Experiencing God* by Henry T. Blackaby and Claude V. King, they write,

> When you believe that nothing significant can happen through you, you have said more about your belief in God than you have said about yourself!

Henry Varley, a friend of D. L. Moody, said, "The world has yet to see what God can do *with*, and *for*, and *through*, and *in* a person who is *fully* and *wholly* consecrated to God!"

Blackaby and King continue by saying, "Varley didn't say we had to be brilliant or highly educated, just a person; an ordinary person."

"IT IS FINISHED!" were the last words Jesus spoke as He gave up His Spirit.

And so it was! And so it is! And so it will be! Death, where is your sting? Grave, where is your victory? Jesus, the Christ, has defeated both!

Father, we thank You that You have not given us the spirit of fear but of *power, love,* and a *sound mind.* And we are convinced and sure of this very thing: that You, Who began a good work in us, will continue it until the day of Christ's return.

I also ask You that somewhere in the pages of this book, even if it is only one sentence, may the reader or listener hear from You! May You speak to their hearts, and in doing so, may they experience getting to know you personally! In Jesus's Name! Amen and Amen!

ABOUT THE AUTHOR

Just A. Nobody was born and raised in Sussex County New Jersey, currently living in Siesta Key, Florida.